Birthright

by

Gerald St Clare

With special thanks to Gordana & David

ISBN: 978-1-64316-151-8

Published by Silversphere Media

A Division of the Sovereign Media Group.

© 2018 All rights reserved

No part of this publication may be reproduced, distributed or transmitted in any form or by any means, including photocopying, recording or other electronic or mechanical methods, without the prior written permission of the publisher, except in the case of brief quotations contained in critical reviews and certain other non-commercial uses permitted by copyright law.

All characters and events portrayed in this work are fictional. Any resemblance to any persons living or dead is purely coincidental.

Birthright

Purity year 0 (Earth year 2988 AD), day 1

Arkship Purity (official designation AS282) had arrived.

After seven hundred and twenty-one years travelling from Earth across the empty void, Purity had reached her symbolic ingression point into the anonymous stellar system. Although she had already been burning her last reserves of fuel for eight months to slow her frantic pace, (with planet fall still more months away), today was considered Arrival Day.

The end of the generations-long journey was to be marked by a magnificent ceremony as the Grande Dame looped around the new sun and headed for her final destination.

♦

Terry Roberts was born to be a butler. Not in any metaphoric sense, no; Terry was actually chosen from the embryo store and trained from birth to serve as a butler for the first Leader of the planet. At his sixteen year examinations, he had successfully outperformed his peers (as predicted by all his teachers) and had been confirmed as First Butler. The pretenders accepted their lower positions, content just to be in service for the First Grand House.

But he hadn't done it alone. From the age of six, he and Deborah Chambers knew that they were better than the other children. They had been as thick as thieves since finding out that their destinies were to be the main care-givers for the most important person on the planet. Deborah was going to be (subject to exam results) nanny to the Leader, so together they saw themselves as surrogate parents - although were never so imprudent as to voice that opinion. Their campaign had been relentless, always differentiating themselves and excluding other children who did not accept subservient roles. Their greatest coup was achieved around the age of ten, when nice old Mr Scarborough agreed that they could wear black instead of the regulation blues. From that day, the pair of them could be mistaken for Manager caste; he in his tailored-look black suits and she in her severe long skirts and jackets. The other children didn't stand a chance.

After his confirmation, Terry had started his apprenticeship with that same Mr Scarborough. Avery Scarborough was only in his late sixties, but as the oldest of the three Managers, he was considered antediluvian by everyone on board. For the last three years Terry had been a part of the furniture during many personal and public interchanges between Mr Scarborough and his team, for which he had cultivated a deep respect for the man. This morning had been a case in point: the most significant date on their journey, a turning point for so many and a start point for all, Mr Scarborough was unflappable. The disastrous loss of his gold cuff links was addressed with a smile and "Put away that shirt, we should do this in dress uniform." Terry had obviously misplaced them, but there was no finger-pointing or recrimination, just a cheerful solution to the problem.

So with his work for the morning done and Mr Scarborough secreted in his office in preparation for the ceremony, Terry stood with his back to the maintenance hall looking out at the stars. Although made to look like a large picture window, the vista was actually a image recorded earlier from the non-rotating part of the ship. As he felt her hand slip into his, Deborah breathed a greeting into his ear. "You look nice."

"Are you sure you're a nanny, not a ninja?" He squeezed her hand back and leaned into her.

They stood together, each pondering if the tiny crescent in the middle of the screen would treat them well.

♦

Avery Scarborough shook his head in disbelief and passed the printout to his second-in-command. Victoria Berengar was surprised at the lack of reverence from the old man, so completely out of character. She took her turn while Ragunath Pande waited with unconcealed impatience.

"We should have guessed he was a bloody hippie. 'Purity' for dung's sake! That was the clue."

Victoria shushed Avery while she finished reading. Ragunath was already pecking at the corner of the paper so she released it with a glare at the young Manager.

Avery carried on with his rant, "And what the hell is an Utu? More like 'Utter stupidity', I'd say."

Ragunath was still reading but interrupted while pointing at a word on the page. "Not 'uhtuh', it's pronounced 'oo-too', Sumerian I think."

Victoria decided to conciliate. "It's just names Avery - and probably with some historical or mythical significance too. What about the main body of the Orders?"

Avery cooled a little. "It's all pretty much consistent. I guess all Leaders want their planets to be some sort of Utopia, so it sort of makes sense."

◆

Proclamation of Claustima Baines-Crackpole for the foundation of Arkship 282 and execution of

planetary license HD20367. Part 3: Leader's Orders Regarding Colony.

I greet you all from your distant past and congratulate you on reaching this important milestone toward the realisation of my vision. Your journey is now all but over and only a few small tasks need to be completed before you can benefit from the bounty that I have bestowed on you.

Firstly I shall attend to the most important issue of Naming: Our sun will be called Utu, after light and balance.

Our planet will be called Purity, after the vessel and the virtue that has brought us so far.

Our first planet fall leader shall be a male heir titled 'Claustima Baines-Crackpole II, First Leader' and I shall heretofore and throughout history be referred to as 'Claustima Baines-Crackpole I, Founder of Homeland Purity'.

Secondly I shall deal with Foundation:

The homeworld planet Purity and all its inhabitants and dominions in the system of

Utu shall remain the property of the Leader in perpetuity.

Our home must be pure and balanced and to this end I proclaim that we will abandon and heretofore abjure all influences that compromise this principle. In the first place: our settlers may use any means necessary to journey to the homeland but on arrival shall permanently destroy any artefacts and technology from the Electric-Age or later. Secondly: construction, maintenance and future development shall be supported only by resources that grow on the land and under the sea; but only in partnership with our environment, never as its master.

I gift to you all a life of gratifying toil for the glory and comfort of the Leader!

(You may toast me now, followed by Claustima Baines-Crackpole II, First Leader.)

As mandated by the Arkship Charter of 2188 and Embarkation Agreements AS282, any person not wishing to accept these terms may depart from the Arkship after repayment of their travelling costs to the Leader. Interest charges and the cost of one personal airlock full of air at 0.1 atm will be waived if the transaction is completed by ingression day.

◆

Avery lowered the proclamation (now printed on thick vellum decorated with watermarks and crests and bearing the heavy red seal of the Crackpole line). He looked over the gathering, not expecting any response. One of the audience started to clap, but that petered out to silence.

The maintenance bay was the largest open space on the arkship and had been converted into a elegant hall through judicious use of paper streamers and the artwork of twenty generations of Managers. The balloons were a disaster, just one flaccid bag hung near the inner door where the staff had forgotten to remove it. But overall it was a suitable display which would be made into an August Occasion for Posterity through video editing. He glanced again at the Orders. "Maybe not."

Forty-six Service personnel stood in a loose congregation in front of Avery while he was flanked by the chairs of Managers Victoria Berengar and Ragunath Pande. Avery snapped his fingers at an apeman standing at the back of the room, who opened the door and a swarm of them came in with glasses of wine for the audience. When all 49 inhabitants of Arkship 282 'Purity' were armed with wine, Avery enacted that last order. "To our Founder, Claustima Baines-Crackpole the First, err, Founder of, umm, Homeland Purity!" All glasses were raised, a few clinked and one or two downed in one. "and to our new Leader, Claustima Baines-Crackpole the Second, First Leader!" Further sipping, more clinking and some unconvincing mime from the empty-glassed ones.

Right at the back of the gathering Terry and Deborah stood hand in hand, lost in private thoughts and completely oblivious to their surroundings other than the nasty sour taste left by the weak vinegar they had just sipped.

Purity Year 0, day 342

Normally the period between their slingshot around the star and planetary arrival was a quiet time for everyone on board an arkship. Automated systems would insert the ship into a high orbit around the destination planet, where it would split and disperse into a hundred or so individual craft. Even settlement selection was out of the hands of the humans; the systems knew the parameters and would select sites for survivability and opportunity and deliver suitable habitats down to those locations. Whether the planet was a sterile ball requiring ten thousand years of terraforming or a lush garden, all the colonists would need to do is read their individual orders and get on a shuttle. Those notes would map out the rest of their lives.

But the Founder clearly wasn't big on detail. The Purity systems were only programmed as far as orbit, which left the problem of how to transform a hostile planet with stone axes entirely to his minions. Under the circumstances, one would expect the three Managers, weighed down with the tasks normally delivered pre-launch by 300 people and a dedicated system, to miss a few details in the short months they had available.

Avery Scarborough addressed the problem as all the greatest managers before him had: he would delegate. The 46 service staff were split equally into two groups: Team A and Team 1 (Ragunath lobbied for 'Team

Vitality' and 'Team Aspiration' and Victoria for either A/B or 1/2, but Avery was having none of it.) Each team member had overall responsibility for one aspect of the colonisation effort, those responsibilities closely aligned with their skill set and normal duties. Team A was a more technical group, so Victoria was in charge of monitoring and managing them, Ragunath delivering the same management role for the more 'social' Team 1. Avery's intention was to incrementally disband team A as their technologies were taken offline and transfer them as subordinates to Team 1 members.

Everyone managed to fit in seamlessly with this plan except Francis May, the geneticist.

Each arkship was basically a factory to recreate Earth on a distant planet. It carried a vault containing the frozen seed for all the plants and animals that would inhabit the new world, including around twenty million fertilised human embryos. During the journey the geneticist was responsible for selecting the appropriate embryos to maintain an in-transit population of around four managers and up to fifty service workers, and ensuring the dormant millions were kept healthy. After terraforming was complete and comfortable living arrangements available, the then working geneticist would also select a range of Leader embryos to become the First Families

With a function so critical to the success of the journey, geneticists often exhibited a God Complex, at the very least believing they were more important than any other service worker. As far as Avery was concerned, Francis May was showing all the signs of this delusion; insisting that he have special dispensation to retain modern technology for a period of at least sixty years following planet fall Now they were entering orbit around the fourth planet, it had all come to a head.

"Do you understand the importance of Leader's Orders Francis?" The little man in Avery's office was hopping around as if on hot coals. He seemed unsure which foot to stand on and was wringing his hands in time to the dance. "Stand still man!"

Avery's words pinned Francis to the floor, as he shoved his hands deep in his pockets and spoke through rigid jaws. "Yes, Mr Scarborough. They must be obeyed to the letter."

"Yes, 'to the letter'. You have the space walk option if you don't like that..."

Already showing signs of resuming his jig. "No, this isn't about me. We can't just bring everyone to term on day one. Even if we had the resources to do that we would end up with a population all of identical age and you must be able to see how unsustainable that is."

Avery felt that the geneticist was bordering on insubordination, but couldn't identify the exact infraction. "If you don't have the skills and knowledge to implement orders, maybe you should spend your last three months training up your replacement."

Francis ignored the threat. "If Leader's Orders said we can't use shuttles to land – or, I don't know, something impossible - what would you do?"

That was just too much for Avery. "You don't question me and you don't disobey the Leader! Find a way or I will." His voice changed to a monotone. "Open." and the door to his office swished open. Francis took the hint and scurried out.

Avery rose and walked over to the Leader Proclamation (Part 3) which was now polyframed and mounted on the wall. He read the offending section "...our settlers may use any means necessary to journey to the homeland but on arrival shall permanently destroy any artefacts and technology from the Electric-Age or later..." Head down and deep in thought he returned to his wing chair. "Settlers. ... any means to journey ... on arrival ..." he repeated. He marvelled at the genius of the leader who had preempted his current problem and placed all the clues in the proclamation!

With a finger on the desk communicator "Call Ragunath Pande".

Ragunath accepted the call while still talking to one of his team. "... summary by tomorrow. Dismissed. Hello Avery, how's it going at the pointy end?"

"It's crawling with big-endians."

"You can't make an omelette without cracking a few."

"Enough, Ragu. I can't keep up." Ragunath waited while Avery paused. "I'd like you to give one of your guys a dispensation."

Ragunath sounded doubtful. "Special Dispensation needs to go through Legal and then have unanimous Manager agreement. It may take some time. Is it our egg-man kicking up a stink again?"

"Yes, it's Francis. But I think he's right with his request. It's a big one but the Leader has already covered it in Orders, so no Legal and all that."

"Sounds good, what's the dispensation?"

Avery carefully delivered each word. "To continue to operate the embryo vault for 60 years following planet fall"

"No! That's ridiculous! What is pre-electric about a hatchery?"

"Just read the orders, Ragu. We aren't the 'settlers', the embryos are. And their journey is not just to orbit, it's to birth. They don't arrive until they are born."

Ragunath still sounded sceptical "Hold on. Calling up my copy." There was a long pause with a few 'hmm's', both of doubt and agreement. "OK, that's really clever of the Leader but don't forget the word 'necessary'. I'll back you up on this provided all unnecessary systems are expired. He's not keeping his coffee maker or getting an air conditioned office."

Avery was certain those extra precautions would ensure Victoria's agreement as well. "Thanks, Ragu. You do your bit, I'll talk to Victoria."

"Aye, aye, skipper!"

Avery winced; he was certain Ragunath would use those stupid phrases in front of a minion one day. He could imagine his hard-won authority dissipating all too easily.

"Ready for some tea, Sir?"

Damn, I forgot the butler was in the anteroom. He's like one of those insects they used to have that always watch you from the corner of the room. "Thank you, Roberts. I suppose it is about that time now."

◆

Victoria Berengar wasn't at all happy. Granted, everything was going well and her team were only getting good news from the planet. But every success was another broken promise, another cherished toy sent for recycling. Her entire life had been dedicated to nurturing and polishing the technical systems on board Putrefy (*I must stop calling it that, she reminded herself. One day I might say it out loud.*). And now her only purpose was abandoning her babies.

Her people had been studying the planets orbiting their destination star for the last five and a half years. The gas giants, their moons and the outer rocky planets were rapidly discounted as too difficult to work with. *Maybe later.* The two nearest planets to the star were tidally locked to it, always showing the same blistering face to the furnace and their freezing backs to the galaxy. They gave the same obstacle to successful colonisation as Mercury back in the 'old system'. The third to fifth all looked good from a distance and as they got closer it was confirmed that all of them were habitable. The Baines-Crackpole system looked like it was going to be a thriving and profitable venture, even if two of the planets were leased to associated families to accelerate the colonisation efforts.

But that was all based on the old standard.

Once the ingression proclamation was read, all bets were off. Although they could start colonies on all three habitable planets before abandoning modern technology, the third did not have a thick enough atmosphere to survive on without a pressure dome and the fifth far too cold for simple wood fires. But before departure, over seven hundred years ago, they had known the fourth planet had an atmosphere breathable without assistance, (which itself was a sign of extensive vegetation), so this was their only chance.

Victoria looked again over the latest environment reports from the drones down on the surface.

With only 35% of the surface covered by water, the land areas should be all desert with only narrow fertile coastal margins where monsoonal winds provided moisture for part of the year. But the place was so green! Right into the deepest interior the landscape was verdant and thriving. The excavators had attacked a small area inland from their preferred first settlement, hacked everything into small pieces and sent the analysis results to her that morning.

"Call Aver..." She was interrupted by swish of her door and an old man walking in without waiting for permission. "... Cancel." Victoria tapped the reports on her desk. "I was just about to call you about these."

Avery helped himself to a seat. "Looking good?"

"Yes, we have wood."

Avery gave her a strange look verging on a smile but said nothing.

She continued. "The whole place is covered with enormous trees; their wood is fibrous (which looks good for building) and their upper roots as hard as Cellform. I'll be dispatching equipment to build lumber yards straight away."

Avery nodded. Better than they could have hoped for. "And minerals?"

Victoria reached over to another pile of reports on a side table. "Tectonic activity is nonexistent so that's a no-go with the stone age kit we are allowed."

"Careful, Victoria, I've warned you about that attitude."

She sneered. "Yes, 'Trust The Leader.'" and passed him the forestry report. "So no ductile materials, but those roots might have some applications.'"

"What about water?"

"The early estimates were right, almost no surface water on the continents and super-deep aquifers." She reached over to the report Avery was holding and flipped to a different page. "But the trees save us again. Those deep roots can act as our osmotic pumps – just tap in and draw all you need." Avery seemed content, but Victoria had a feeling that he hadn't actually visited for an update on the reports. "And?"

"I need your approval for something."

"Mine? When did I get to be Leader?"

"It's just something we need to be unanimous on. Ragu and I have agreed to let the geneticist keep his vault for a couple of generations. I need your vote."

Victoria didn't even think about it. "Yeah, not a problem." Then with a faraway look. "But he'll need generators, fuel and a load of other stuff to support it."

Avery wasn't going to fall for that. "This isn't a license for a technology base, Victoria. Just necessary services. I don't want you building oil wells and tractor factories. Just one solar array to power his refrigeration and splicing equipment. Anything else not already in his vault gets cut off and decommissioned."

Victoria reverted to that resigned look he had seen all too often over the last few weeks.

Purity Year 1, day 29

Deborah was under no illusion as to who was senior here. Francis may be the Geneticist and this may be the GenLab, but he was just a convenient stepping stone to Her Glory. He was little different to the teachers whose opinions she had suffered in her younger years, just a resource to be mined. The man was so petty that he had printed up that stupid "GenLab 2" sign to stick on the door when his unit was transferred down to the planet.

Today the little toad was treating her like a cleaner! But despite the ignominy, Deborah finished her tasks with complete dedication. The little chamber she had sterilised so assiduously was to be the womb for the most important living person for the entire history of planet Purity. *What a beautiful name* she mused *pure as the heart of a Leader and cleaned of all polluting influences. The Leader has truly given us a small piece of his own perfection.*

"All done, Mister May." The last part forced out with difficulty. *That little shit has no right to insist on being addressed like a Manager. Mister indeed!*

"Thank you Deborah, I can always rely on you." Francis May appeared, still pulling on a pair of powder blue Latexeen gloves. "Would you like to hit the button?"

Deborah was taken aback. 'The Button' was just the 'OK' on the screen at the GenLab desk, but Francis knew as well as she what it represented. Once the system was given the Okay to proceed, it would reach into the cryogenic vault, select the correct embryo from the Baines-Crackpole family and transport it to its mechanical womb. She couldn't believe that Francis May would cede the birth of the Leader to her! She nodded humbly and walked to the screen. As she approached,

Francis mimicked a herald holding an oversized trumpet and sang "Ta-ra-rah! Ta-ra-rah!"

She punched the screen and stepped back in confusion. "Bastard!"

Francis didn't realise she was referring to him. "What's wrong?"

Deborah mumbled slowly, clearly repeating words with no meaning. "dee bee sea four oh six one three refer to systems".

Francis cheered up. "DBC. That's just the blue cable. It falls out because the little spigot has broken off. I get DBC's and WAN's every time I run a vacuum cleaner round here." He had already stooped below the main console and was fiddling with the equipment. From the hidden depths: "Hit it again."

Deborah realised this may not be a ploy to diminish her after all, so checked the screen again. "The OK has gone."

The invisible voice was starting to sound impatient. "Clear the error message and restart the process."

He might as well have spoken to her in Njerip, she tapped the screen again and again but nothing changed. "What's the process?"

Francis reappeared and hustled her out of the way. "Oh, I see what you mean. Sorry, Deborah. I'll sort it out." He reached for the desk communicator, then remembering it had been disabled after the last shuttle had landed, withdrew his hand and wandered out of the main entrance.

Deborah tapped the screen one more time, then sat back staring at it as though her force of will would make everything fine.

♦

The early morning humidity had already dissipated, sucked out of the air within minutes of the sun breaking through the low inversion. Francis May had no experience of the forests and jungles of old Earth, so found no incongruity in the combination of a dense canopy and air so dry that you felt like you had needles growing inside your nose. GenLab itself was under open skies in an artificial clearing about eight hundred metres in diameter, but Francis was already on the forest track to the support unit where he would be able to "refer to systems" as the message had so helpfully instructed.

In all his twenty-two ship-bound years, the ground had been uniform and uncompromisingly hard, the air quality precisely controlled for temperature and humidity, the light was always grey and either on or off. In contrast, a walk on Purity (the planet) was a symphony for the senses he could hardly have imagined; a thousand different smells drifted past while bright blooms of every hue shouted their invitations for insect visitors. But it wasn't easy. Granted, all the crew had spent the previous few years working on strength and stamina, so this generation were larger and much fitter than any of those destined to live and die in the cocoon. But his joints! The unevenness and undulation of the surface was twisting his ankles mercilessly and putting torsional forces on his knees that made him think they would unscrew like a jar lid. *Thank Newton there aren't any hills to speak of!* He walked on with his joints crackling in time with the detritus on the path.

As the systems unit came into sight ahead, Francis felt an uneasy emptiness around him. The Diesel generator was no longer running (as planned, although a little earlier than he would have expected), but there was a deeper silence too – as though everyone had shut up shop and left. At the actual door, that impression was complete. The airlock was closed and didn't respond to "Open" voice activation or a physical bash on the glass (the standard emergency entry procedure). He pressed his nose to the port and saw that the inner door was closed too, so impossible to see if anyone was inside. As he stepped back, a note fluttered to the ground and lay there "butter side up".

There on the ground, a little cartoon running man with dreadlocks streaming behind him was carrying a sign, "NGB". One of Mr Pande's "No Going Back" motivational stickers that were placed on all decommissioned equipment.

♦

Victoria Berengar always had something of a soft spot for Francis Avery, intrigued by his single-minded purpose. She speculated that he had one of those brain disorders where one is dissociated from human interaction and lives in a word of things and actions. Of course, such maladies had been weeded out of the population a long, long time ago; but she preferred that to Avery's idea that Francis was just an annoying little wannabe megalomaniac.

But today he was testing her patience.

"It just doesn't work like that Miss Berengar."

She couldn't see why he was making such a big thing of it. "Just go to the section where the Crackpoles are stored and pick one at random then."

"You do understand the principle of redundancy?"

She gave him a withering look. Criticising a superior was a zeroing offence. But she didn't actually understand the context. "Of course I do, but I suspect you don't Francis."

He seemed to fall for that. "Everything is randomly distributed, so loss of any location will not take out a complete service. That's not just for ship systems, we organise the seed vault the same way. Each family is spread out across the vault – randomly. You can't just go to a 'Berengar' section or a 'May' section."

Victoria stepped through the details mentally. Slowly her appreciation of the problem started to catch up with Francis'. "And you don't have a local database?" But already knowing the answer, she showed Francis her palm. No response necessary. "Who knows about this?"

"Well, the systems people will know they broke it. And the nanny was there when the error message came up. She's quite bright so will probably work it out. And you and me."

But damage limitation was not really an option. This could be a terminal problem for the whole planet. "So Francis, what can I do to help you fix this?"

No hesitation. "Get the database back online."

"That's gone Francis. The hardware, the backups, everything. It's gone. Is there any way you can reverse engineer? Maybe test until you find a Leader?"

Francis seemed to escape into that world of things and actions, his eyes drifted upward and he mouthed silent words. Finally and with no real conviction, he proposed "I can use swabs from our current population and DNA match to embryos. Given enough time, I could identify all the 'Berengars', 'Averys', 'Mays' and so on."

"We aren't the Leaders, Francis. How would you identify the Crackpoles?"

"Only by getting the database online."

Purity Year 1, day 30

Francis was under strict orders to be available but hear nothing. The latter was impossible as he was sitting in a small room with the three Managers, but he reasoned that if he said nothing, he could argue that he heard nothing. Old Mr Scarborough and the two younger Managers, Miss Berengar and Mr Pande were in the middle of a heated discussion, a sight that was to him, almost surreal.

"I have to be honest, Victoria, you've made a total Goethe of this." Avery was trying hard not to explore his suspicion that the other Manager had deliberately given them a setback to prove her point.

"Me? You are the one who jumped in with Mr Crackpot's scheme. And then you think a nursery can run standalone?"

Before Avery could respond, Ragunath cut in. The crackpot-Crackpole slur was definitely in Termination territory. "People! We need to move forward. No recriminations. No Going Back!" The resulting united hostility from the other two gave Ragunath a small sense of achievement.

Avery turned on him. "And with no way forward? What do we do then?"

Victoria had already given it more thought than the two men had. "If May starts his testing, he can give us embryos that are definitely not related to anyone currently in service, including the three of us. The Leaders must be in that group, so if we pick one of those at random we might get a Leader." She looked to Francis for confirmation but he just averted his gaze to a small section of door frame.

Ragunath had no doubt about the protocol. "No. We can't risk a Manager or Service caste family accidentally becoming Leader. If that ever gets out, there would be a revolution like you wouldn't believe."

Victoria was not giving up. "What about an interim Leader? Wasn't there something in the Contingencies covering that?"

Ragunath was now in his area of expertise. "Yes, for homeworlds that require extensive terraforming. To save the Leader families from suffering centuries in Habitats, long terraform worlds allow for interim leadership. Not. And I stress "Not". interim Leaders."

Avery sounded impatient. "That's just hair-splitting. What's the difference between an interim Leader and interim leadership?"

Ragunath pretended not to be offended, carefully replying. "An interim Leader would be a person. Interim leadership is provided by a robot. Usually a GV30 series programmed to implement Leaders Orders as already written."

Victoria dusted her hands together. "All good then. Roll out a GV32, I'll get it loaded up and off we go."

"Wait!" Avery saw the last hole in the plan. "And why are we using an interim Leader?"

"...ership." Ragunath helpfully added.

Victoria was nonplussed. "Did you even hear what we were talking about?"

Avery gave a 'calm down' wave of his hand. "What do we tell everyone else? Why are we activating a contingency? What is the penalty for the balls-up we have just presided over?"

Victoria saw the light. "Ah, yes. Termination. All our descendants are written right here in our genes to be tracked down and Terminated." On Arkships, the penalty for in-transit crimes were draconian.

But Ragunath was all smiles as he reproduced an ancient dance with rigid arms. "So what about a human robot so nobody knows?"

Victoria shook her head, not quite sure why she felt like smiling at such a dire time. "You bloody idiot, Ragu."

Purity Year 1, day 32

Deborah admitted she would have thought any design of Terry's was good, but this one was outstanding.

From where their afternoon picnic was laid out at the eastern edge of the bowl, she could see most of the inner grounds of the estate, with only the central smoothbark forming an obstruction. That unfeasibly gigantic tree rose from who-knows-how-deep to over a hundred metres above the gardens. Originally, the area had all been level at about the altitude she was sitting, but Terry had ordered excavation of a perfect circle centred on the smoothbark, down to a depth of twenty metres. The exposed tangle of large roots, now above ground level, would form a natural framework for the Leader's palace with the crown of the tree giving an hour or so of midday shade. Smaller outcrops of root marred the even surface, but Terry had assured her that these had been deliberately left to form the source and structure for the water features he had planned.

The later excavations were being made by hand (the heavy equipment decommissioned the previous week), and a team of six apemen were working just down the slope digging holes for the beech avenue which, from the palace, would frame the rising sun. In the name of Utu (or balance) the setting sun would be blessed by a matching beech avenue to the west, but that was for another day.

Deborah gave a contented smile as Terry trudged up the slope towards her. He grinned back when he noticed her looking at him. "May I join you, Milady?"

She feigned shock. "Oh, you Roberts men are so forward!"

"Only when there are Chambers ladies around." He planted himself next to her on the blanket and slipped an arm around her waist. "So what do you think?"

"Nice and tingly." she purred.

"No, the palace grounds!"

"Ha ha, I know. They are amazing. I love the way you've woven the 'before' and 'after' together. Just the way The Founder would have wanted it."

Terry's mood switched abruptly. "Such a shame it's all just a waste of time."

Deborah hadn't shared the problem in GenLab with Terry yet, so she was intrigued as to what he meant. "Why?"

"The Managers and the weasel were round at Mr Scarborough's office today..."

"...Don't call him a weasel, Terry. He did something really nice for me on Einsday."

"Well, anyway. It looks like they've lost all the Leaders."

Deborah made the connection. "Oh, that's what it was."

"It?"

"Yes. When we tried to select the leader for birth, the vault went doolally."

Terry gave her a little poke in the ribs. "Doolally? Is that a technical term you've picked up from your new friends?"

"Stop that Terry. I think I did something to break the vault."

"No, not you. The Managers said it was the systems people who broke it. Now they have millions of eggs and they only know 46 families out of thousands." (Terry could be forgiven for not getting the numbers quite right). "They can't hatch anyone to lead in case its a Service or Manager."

Deborah shuddered at the thought of a mere Manager being Leader, let alone a true 'pleb'. The whole place would fall apart! "So what did they decide?"

"Nothing. They need a clone."

That made no sense to Deborah. "A clone? You still need a Leader egg for a clone."

Terry accepted his mistake. "No, not a clone. The human robot thing."

"A cyborg?" Deborah was doubtful that would help.

"Yes. A cyborg that is so convincing that everyone thinks it's a human Leader."

"I think you mean 'android', Terry. Cyborgs are the other way round."

"Ooh, so who's an expert on replicants now? Could you make me one?"

Deborah was not to be distracted by his playful sarcasm.

"Maybe I can." Deep in thought, she looked down the hill at the workers.

◆

Avery's first impression was that the young man had come to ask 'her father's permission'. Two smartly dressed young people had arrived at his office and sheepishly asked if they could talk with him about a delicate matter. The boy was his butler, Terry Roberts; the girl had a face that might have been pretty if it didn't exhibit a combination of fear and severity. Based on her age and the way she was tightly attached to Terry's arm, he guessed she was the nanny.

"Yes, of course Roberts. Bring her in." Avery gallantly shifted the position of a chair by five millimetres. "Here, have a seat young lady."

Deborah looked to Terry doubtfully. Managers weren't supposed to treat you like honoured guests. Terry just nodded to her as though it was all perfectly normal, so she settled in the chair.

"A delicate matter you say?" Avery was delighted that he might be announcing the settlement's first natural birth. "When is it due?" He asked conspiratorially.

Terry was alarmed. "No, no, no. Nothing like that! It's about the vault problem. Miss Chambers here may have a solution for you."

Miss Chambers? Terry was stepping over the line there on the Manager/Service boundary. Avery decided to humour them. "You were there when the geneticist tried to pull the Leader egg?"

Deborah nodded. "Embryo. Yes."

"And you can fix the system?"

"No. But I can give you an android."

Avery realised where she had got that information. So spider man talks to the nanny. "And how will you do that Deborah?"

"You need an empty vessel that looks like a person. One that can pretend to be a Leader. I think I can bring an apeman up thinking he is a Leader. That could buy us thirty years to find the real Leaders."

Avery was determined not to humiliate her. "It's very nice of you to try and help, but nobody will find 'Ugh, ugh, ugh' a particularly inspiring speech. And cutlery! It won't just be a case of using the correct spoon, he'll be shoving his whole face in the soup."

Terry had to step in. "I'm sorry to interject sir, but there is a precedent. On Old Earth, Quentin Fortenberry ran AllCorp for twenty years and never once appeared at a formal occasion. They say the only reason they got the candid shots of him was PR to prove he actually existed."

Deborah put her hand on Terry's. She gave him a look that said. *I can look after myself.* "I can do better than that Mr Avery. Give me an apeman at an impressionable age and I can guide his life."

Purity Year 1, day 34

Back in those first days when Avery Scarborough and Ragunath Pande were running around trying to realise the Founder's dream of a sylvan Utopia, Victoria Berengar had other plans.

Victoria was a tech-head through and through; spending hours working on a frannistan or reading about the inner workings of some interesting gadget. Despite this, she was almost willing to accept the loss of all current hardware because of the promise of a new mission to rediscover lost technologies. Only the previous week she had learned about the need for dwell angles when casting metals – such intricacies showed her that Old Engineering could be as detailed and complicated as anything current.

But that realisation brought with it a deeper understanding of the problem. Whether making cartwheels or space stations, one has to 'stand on the shoulders of giants'.

The ship library was a digital collection of tens of millions of books, papers, articles as well as fiction and cultural documents. Avery was already in the process of organising the steam-powered wood-block printing presses which would transcribe a tiny part of this treasure to paper, but Victoria knew that was a waste of time. How could three Managers decide which two hundred books contained all the human knowledge they would ever need? She was not as naive as those ancient people who thought Johannes Gutenberg could have stopped after his first book. It simply wasn't possible to predict the entire future history of a planet based on a meeting of the elite.

So she cheated.

In her role as technical director, Victoria truly believed she could decide what was necessary and compliant with Leader's Orders without involving the others. Their lack of understanding of the problem would just be a distraction and obstacle to proper preparation. A digital copy of the library had to be saved.

Her options were limited. The only facility that would have the hardware and power she needed for the foreseeable future was Francis May's unit. Pulling a backup stack from the library was easy, but she needed an excuse for basing herself and her equipment in GenLab. After days of prevarication, she had an idea; a weak argument but she would have to see if she could con Avery and Ragunath into agreeing.

"Avery, I need your approval to..."

He didn't even turn from the two blue-suited assistants who were stacking pallets onto the disposal shuttle. "Approval, approval, approval. Can't you just get on with it Victoria? You're supposed to be a Manager!"

"Umm, but..."

"Oh, I know. I'll stop what I'm doing and make up a rubber stamp 'Approved'. Do your damned job Victoria!" *No need for a cover story then. She was bewildered but walked away content.*

◆

Francis May had doubts about the plan, both in its effectiveness and the moral position. Admittedly, over the years he had argued a number of points with each of them, but the idea that one would ever disobey a Manager's request was completely alien to him. So keeping it all a secret from the two younger Managers was, for him, a balancing act between responsibility and guilt.

He was unsure why Mr Scarborough had involved Deborah and Terry in the scheme, maybe a necessary part of their onboarding to his department. But they were both nice, well mannered young people so he was sure they would all make a good team.

They told him that he needed to select an apeman embryo to act as interim leader until he worked out who the real Leaders were. That first part was a really easy task as he always had at least half a dozen of those cooking due to their high attrition rate. Right now, he actually had almost thirty in gestation chambers in preparation for the extra deaths that planetary labour would incur. Francis selected one of these wombs, peeled off the sticker "D4267/1412(M)" and carefully positioned a handwritten "A1/1(M)" sticker in its place.

There was a a gentle footfall behind him, he whirled round in alarm. *Miss Berengar! Did she see what I just did?*

She smiled kindly. "It will take some time to adjust to sharing your space, Francis. But you don't need to panic, I don't bite." She spotted the handwriting on the gestation chamber and pushed past him for a closer look. "You found a Leader egg?"

"Err, Yes. Just found one."

"Without the database. How?" She was peering intently at the fluid sac containing a little curled up person behind the Flexglass.

"Testing." He sounded really uncertain.

Suspicious that this "new" embryo was probably already three months old, Victoria Berengar turned and saw guilt written all over his disposition. She reached down and opened his hand to retrieve a screwed-up scrap of something. The answer was neatly printed right there in front of her. "D. Service? I'm guessing 4267 is the May family?"

Francis May was horrified at the accusation. "No, I wouldn't..." He rushed to the line of occupied chambers, pointing at the labels. They all started with 'D4267'. "It's not Service, it's the apeman line." He rushed to the door near to panic and called loudly. "Cleaner! Here, Now!"

An orange-clad individual shambled in within seconds and Francis pointed to her chest badge bearing the same designation, D4267/1367. "Where, Sir?" She asked.

"Oh, just do the floor."

Victoria said nothing while the apeman went through the motions of sweeping the already antiseptically clean floor. Francis seemed to wither by the minute like a plum under the grill. As the apeman bowed and turned to leave Victoria growled at Francis. "Why?"

"Interim leader until we can find a real Leader." His monotone suggested he was quoting someone elses words.

"Who knows?"

Francis really didn't want to say. "Mmm."

"Who knows!"

"Mister Scarborough, Miss Deborah and Terry Roberts." The geneticist looked like he was in agony.

"And Ragunath. Mr Pande?"

"No."

That took some of the heat out of Victoria. Francis twitched, like he was going to make a run for it. She held up one finger and he froze like the statue of a sprinter in the blocks. "You said it would be impossible to find the Leaders without the database."

"Yes, Miss Berengar. I did."

"So how will this help?"

"I don't know Miss Berengar. Mr Scarborough will know."

Victoria had no time for blind faith. *Avery knows nothing. But he has found us a robot. And protected Ragu and I from Termination. The old man is actually a bit of a gem.*

Francis had no idea why the Manager was smiling to herself. He suspected there was some electrical equipment and soft parts involved in her thoughts.

Purity Year 6, day 198

"Come on Clo' we have to go." Deborah rushed in with a purple cape and held it out for the boy who was still sitting on the floor surrounded by toy soldiers. With a 348 day year, his Purity age of nearly five years was actually only about four and a half earth years. This small discrepancy always made Deborah think that Purity children were far too immature for their ages.

Claustima Baines-Crackpole II, First Leader was not ready to cooperate. "Aya?"

"Yes, Clo'" Deborah closed in on him.

"When I'm big, can we have a war?"

"Why would you want a war, Clo'? Everything is yours and everyone loves you." She tried to surreptitiously slip the cape over his shoulders. He shrugged it to the floor but stood up.

"But I have soldiers."

Picking the cape up, she tried to herd him towards the exit. "Yes. Your army is bigger and stronger than anything within four light-years." *A small point that it was comprised of just 120 four year old part-timers armed with wooden swords, but they'll be trained up in time for any parades.*

"So we can kill all the baddies?"

She agreed "Yes, all the baddies." And finally he was moving in the right direction.

Claustima Baines-Crackpole II, First Leader straightened up to his full three feet seven inches and allowed his Aya, Deborah Chambers to place his ceremonial cape. "I shall tell Vicky to make me bombs for the war."

"That'll be nice." Deborah was reasonably certain that would all be forgotten long before he next saw Victoria Berengar.

Suddenly the boy spotted a well dressed man in his thirties approaching from the front entrance. He barrelled into him, hugging him furiously. "Wobbles!"

Terry Roberts, prised the child off himself then knelt down and adjusted the boy's cravat. "Thank you Sir. A pleasure to see you too." He checked the room, *nobody looking*, and gave Claustima a quick hug back.

"Where are we going, Wobbles?"

Terry had deliberately not warned Claustima about the upcoming event, but Deborah knew how to handle it. "We are going to see Mr Scarborough off."

Claustima turned and gave her a dark look. "Avery smells." he declared.

Unflustered, Deborah replied. "Not any more, Clo'. And this is the last time you will have to see the nice

Mr Scarborough. No more presents and no more funny stories. You just need to say goodbye today so all your subjects are not so sad. They loved Mr Scarborough almost as much as they love you."

"No more presents? He's dead isn't he?" The question was unemotional.

Terry joined in again. "Remember how all your subjects depend on you to help them through difficult times like funerals? Mr Scarborough looked after them all until you came along, so today is important to show everyone that you are really the Leader here. Can you do this for us?"

Claustima had tried to concentrate on what Terry said, but only got that everyone would go soppy and boring if he didn't do it. It was always like that and trusting Terry usually got him through it unscathed. He slipped his hand into Terry's and nodded.

The butler gave an uncertain look to the nanny. She just smiled back, took Claustima's other hand and the pair of them marched out to the carriage, with Claustima using them as a makeshift swing.

♦

In olden times back on Earth, the press would say of a society event 'Everyone was there'; meaning, of course, that all the important people had shown up. At Avery Scarborough's funeral the words were the same, but the meaning different. All four hundred or so human beings over one year old on the entire planet were in attendance. And unlike an Earth-based funeral where a disproportionate number of the congregation would be of elder years, the age distribution here suggested the deceased might be the headmaster of a nursery school.

Central Planning always knew that living on a planet would be a difficult transition for a population brought up in a low-gee antiseptic environment, so shipboard birth rates had been adjusted for the previous century to ensure that when Arrival Day came there would be few with the additional challenge of old age. Under normal circumstances, old Managers like Avery would have lived out the remainder of their days, at zero gee, up on the orbiting Arkship (or at least one of its separated units), but the Proclamation of Claustima the First made that impossible.

Avery had landed with all the other colonists, never complaining about the continual pain and side effects from parts of his anatomy that simply shut down when they experienced the new environment. He kept it together for four years before walking became impossible, from that point carrying out the business of the colony from his bedroom.

And now he was gone.

Ragunath Pande was pleased with the effect that he had achieved. By using the south-east slope of the palace bowl for seating, the congregation were not yet in sunlight, afflicted by the remains of cool, damp early morning mist. But their view over the burial site was backdropped by the magnificent palace which blended seamlessly into the grand smoothbark that rose so high above them that it appeared to reach over and behind them. The burial site itself had been chosen and arranged by Terry Roberts, who had continued to serve Avery even after his apprenticeship ended. That man had been run ragged between Avery's unit and the palace ever since the Leader had vetoed his request to move Avery into a palace apartment.

The Certified Artist was already sketching his interpretation of the scene for the official pictures. Ragunath peered over the artist's shoulder and was unimpressed.

Just as the first rays of sun fell on the heads in the front row, the school band began an interesting version of Widor's Toccata and Fugue in D Minor. With only strings and woodwind, the rendition was passable, particularly from half-scale musicians.

The reason for their activity now became evident: the Grand Carriage of Claustima Baines-Crackpole II, First Leader came into sight around a buttress of the palace. Drawn by two white Andalusions with dancing hooves and flicking tails, the pumpkin-shaped cart travelled the hundred and fifty metres from the palace door to the end of a blood red carpet.

There was a slight hesitation, then the door was thrown wide open in a grand gesture and the First Leader himself appeared, saluted the congregation and shouted "Light!" Immediately the whole throng gave the appropriate response. "And Balance!"

The orchestra took their cue (having fallen silent at the appearance of the leader) and started the first bars of Mozart's Lacrimosa. Claustima II seemed deeply touched by the music, dropping his head in sorrow. But within seconds he rose invigorated, motioned for the music to stop and declared to all his subjects. "From this day forth we shall have no more funerals."

The whole audience erupted in applause while the conductor switched his orchestra in fits and starts to some generic Irish Jig music (all diddly-dah as far as Ragunath was concerned). Before they were all playing in unison, the carriage was already moving away and back round to the hidden front door of the palace.

Amazing statesmanship. Ragunath was in awe of their young Leader. *A credit to his lineage. I'm so glad the geneticist managed to find a way of identifying Leader eggs. Where would we be now with a robot stand in?*

♦

"Let's see my horses!" Claustima was not going to settle in his place, already standing on the front seat and looking out of the small window used to give the driver orders.

Deborah, who he was practically climbing over, tried to soothe him. "Your two best horses are pulling the carriage, Clo'. We are just going round the corner then you can give them a formal inspection for everyone to see. They'll be so proud of you."

"I don't want those. I want to see the brown one with the big willy." He could see he had shocked Deborah, despite her best efforts to hide it.

Terry came to her rescue. "He's at the racecourse Sir. Once the grooms have him ready you can watch him running. We need to give them about twenty minutes so that he doesn't look shabby. You don't like scruffy horses do you? Like those working ones the ordinary people use?"

Claustima had to agree with that. "No, my horses are better than theirs. I have all the best horses."

"Yes. You do indeed, Sir."

The short exchange had got them from the main entrance of the palace, round the herb gardens and now the driver was carefully parking at the end of the red carpet. Claustima jumped to the window and peered out at the crowd. "What are they doing?"

"That's the funeral, Sir. You just need to wave at everyone then we can go down and say goodbye to Mr Scarborough."

"Avery smells and dead things stink. I want to go to the racecourse. No funeral." He sat back, arms crossed in defiance.

Then Terry made a rare tactical mistake. "If you won't do this, you'll have to tell all those people why."

Unsurprisingly, Claustima took that as a challenge. He jumped up and flung the carriage door open. As he stood at the portal, a shaft of sunlight flashed between the cedars on the upper slope and hit him between the eyes. The boy angrily covered his face and shouted a complaint to Terry. He was drowned out by the crowd chanting something - to which he became incandescent with rage. With tears streaming down his face, he ordered the unappreciative peasants. "No more funerals!" and dived back into the carriage to hide his shame. As they drove back to the palace, he could hear them all out there laughing at him.

Purity Year 16, day 347

Deborah watched the young man, wishing she could do something, anything, to ease his suffering.

She had ceased to be his Aya many years ago, and now he saw her as a mere servant. From that position it was impossible to offer the companionship or support that the desperately lonely fifteen year old craved.

The fault was partly of her making. When she first conceived him (yes, she really saw it that way), she should have made sure that children from the other High Families were also brought into the world. In hindsight, that sounded obvious and simple, but even now she had no idea how they might have simulated such a thing.

Claustima was perched on a loop of a smoothbark root waving a riding crop at the ranks of teenagers on his lawns. "It's supposed to be a war you idiot. If you don't hit her hard you won't kill her." He jumped down and stalked to where one of his soldiers was standing over a uniformed girl cowering on the grass. Claustima drew back his weapon and gave the girl a solid whack on the back of the head. She immediately started bawling uncontrollably as a thick red stream of blood oozed down her neck. The boy soldier jumped back in horror, for which he received a hateful look from his Leader.

"All useless!" And Claustima stormed off toward the palace.

Deborah waited until Claustima was out of sight then ran to the weeping girl. Nobody else had moved a muscle. She dragged her own jacket off and wadded it to staunch the flow of blood. "I hope you understood his lesson there, young lady."

The girl gave no response, just sobbing gently.

"What about you?" Deborah looked to the failed assailant accusingly.

The boy swallowed, looked around at his peers for support but knew he was on his own. "That as soldiers, we have to do things that are difficult, ma'am?"

"Difficult? Why was that difficult?" Deborah was relentless.

"Because I'm, err, weak? Because I'm weak?"

"Yes, toughen up young man. You're in the army. Start acting like it." Deborah turned to return to the palace and almost walked into Victoria Berengar.

"He's right. My feeling is that it's actually a Sun Tzu lesson. 'The general shall follow the orders of his sovereign, to which his own principles shall not be an obstruction.'"

Deborah felt there was something all too clever about Miss Berengar. *Wherever does she trawl all those quotes up from? I bet they're just made up for the occasion.*

Victoria walked straight past Deborah and addressed the lines of soldiers. "I need a strong volunteer to help me organise a construction team. You there with the blood and muscles!" She pointed at the girl who scrambled to pick up a bloody black cloth and reapply it to a wound on her head. "You are now head of the Corps of Engineers. Clean yourself up and get down to GenLab!"

The girl gave Victoria a confused look.

Victoria addressed the 'weak soldier'. "Help her up man! Get her checked over at the quack and look after her until she's ready to start work with me. And can someone please say 'fallout' or whatever you trolls need in order to go and have your supper."

Victoria winked at Deborah and received a grateful smile in return.

Purity Year 17, day 22

With its ubiquitous forests, the planet Purity could almost have been designed for the vision of the long gone Founder, Claustima Baines-Crackpole I. Granted, their new planet contains about the same proportion of radioactive material and other useful minerals as Earth, but without the stirring of tectonic activity, the heavy elements are mostly buried hundreds to thousands of kilometres under the surface. Any other arkship would have ignored this fourth planet altogether and settled on either the third or fifth, both of which were far more suitable for getting an industrial society up and running, but the Founder's wishes had put paid to those options.

The legacy of hundreds of millions of years of constant tree cover was written all the way down through the soil. Standing at the edge of the huge chasm, Terry could read that history as his eyes traced the path from the lip, deep down into the maw.

Directly under the carpet of crackling bark and leaves on which he stood, the humus became steadily darker and denser. This formed a metre or so of crumbling overhang all the way around the crater, supported by a line of peat about twelve metres thick. Although it was difficult to tell exactly where it happened, the black soil began to sparkle slightly until right down at the first man-made terrace in the pit, metal beasts gnawed at a face of solid coal.

With a local cloud of choking black smoke and coal dust surrounding each of these steam-powered behemoths it was difficult to see the detail, but Terry could just make out the tail of the nearest machine weaving to the cliff face where a bucket-lift accepted most of that coal, pulling it up to a dispersal point for transportation away. A small proportion of the spoils were diverted back to the machine to feed it continuously during its eighty hour plus working shifts.

At the level where the coal scrapers were standing, there was a sharp change from black to a ruddy sand colour. The floor of this first terrace gave evidence of an epoch when there was little or no plant life in this area. The settlers had no idea how the current profusion of life had so suddenly arisen from a bare landscape of silicates and rocks bearing impoverished quantities of light metals, but they were right there to take advantage of that desolate antiquity.

Deep down on the second terrace Terry knew there was a team of ore scrapers. The only visible evidence of these machines were the tails of coal running over the lower lip to feed them and the dark brown cloud of smoke mixed with dust which seethed like an infernal ground mist all the way to the coal miners. Maybe some of those bucket lifts were raising ore rather than coal, but Terry could not distinguish one from another.

The scene rapidly blurred in the smoggy distance, so it was impossible to make out the far side of the hole, some six kilometres away. That was the static face, where digging had first commenced and the smelters and metal works stood. The mine had grown (and was still growing) from that side towards Terry and to his left and right, all to provide raw materials for the industrial complex.

And the purpose of the factory area? To process all that bounty in order to produce more mining machinery.

Miss Berengar had said that the mines would soon be in surplus so they would be able to move to the production of cannons and armour until the colony was sufficiently defended. And then it would be just a few short years before they could start building palaces for the ruling families.

Everyone would be happy because they would have jobs for decades to come.

Purity Year 19, day 226

"So you've done nothing for twenty-odd years?" Terry was aghast at Francis May's attitude.

Francis wasn't going to give any ground. "Do you not understand what the word 'impossible' means?"

Terry charged forward, ending up with his nose a millimetre from Francis' "Did you say 'incompetent'? Yes, I think you're giving me a nice demonstration of the meaning."

"Boys." Deborah's tone was that gently chiding sound of a nanny coming between two children. Grown men have no defence, so both stepped back. She had a deep thoughtful look as she turned to Francis. "You can test the genetic makeup of embryos, right?"

"I can sequence the entire DNA chain once the blastomer is big enough to survive the test."

Terry shrugged and turned to Deborah. "What did he just say?"

"He said only after they are incubated." Deborah continued her interrogation. "So if you pull a random selection and incubate them, you could compare DNA for that group."

"Of course. I do that for every child. I have records for every birth since planetfall I also have the same records from swabs taken from the 49 families who landed."

"So if you just keep testing, eventually you will find an embryo with perfect DNA."

Warning bells were flashing in Francis' head as he heard the code words. *That damned Eugenics movement had a lot to answer for! 'Perfect DNA' indeed!* He wasn't going to even start that conversation with her if she subscribed to that lunacy. "Of the sixteen thousand records so far, half a dozen families are showing marginally less genetic disorders."

Terry couldn't contain his excitement. "There! Those are the First Families!"

Deborah raised a calming hand. "And is there one that stands out?"

Francis could see where this was going, both in her head and in reality. "Yes, absolutely. One family shows marginally more resilience than all the others and usually grows up with lower incidence of congenital disease."

Deborah dusted her hands in an excellent imitation of the Manager Miss Berengar. "That wasn't so hard, was it?"

"Yes, simple reasoning generally gets an answer more quickly." Francis suspected they missed his sarcasm.

As the couple left, Francis was still ruminating on the fact that if he had reversed their logic, he may actually have found the Leaders: the most inbred families would show the most severe genetic damage. He had simply been blinded to that solution by his adulation of his superiors. Unfortunately, the differences would still be impossible to identify with the small sample and limited time he had available.

Francis finished the new sticker "A1/3(M)" and picked a male heir at random from the one family he already knew had the 'most perfect' DNA. "Goodbye apeman D4267/3644(M), hello Claustima Baines-Crackpole the Third."

Purity Year 20, day 32

Of all the people on planet Purity, the First Leader had no greater trust for any person than he had for Terry Roberts. The role of the butler was so ingrained in Claustima Baines-Crackpole II's life that Terry was not just a right-hand man, he was a more integrated part than Claustima's own arm. And this trust, founded in dependency, caused Claustima to be devoid of suspicion at any of Terry's suggestions. Anyone else was treated as a potential aggressor; offers of delicacies scorned as poisoning attempts, invitations to join a group as strategy to gang up on him; Claustima had secluded himself behind a wall of paranoia. So Terry's suggestion of a secret and surprise outing offered mystery and excitement that Claustima had largely excluded himself from.

"I'll need wine Roberts. Bring some of the Syrah, it's almost drinkable."

"I think I might even join you in a tipple today Sir; maybe a couple of bottles."

"Good man, Roberts! It's about time you let loose some of that stuffiness. Maybe I can get you drunk enough to laugh at some of my jokes." Claustima watched Terry selecting something from the cabinet. "You can laugh at that too, you know!"

"Yes Sir, very droll." Terry seemed satisfied with the reflections from a pair of crystal wine glasses and rolled them up in napkins. "We should open them here, Sir. The '08 was quite capricious."

"'Capricious', eh? You mean half the time it tastes like piss! Yes, crack them open until we get a couple of good ones."

Terry had already lined up four additional glasses and was in the process of opening the first bottle. He poured half a glass and took it over to Claustima. By the time

Claustima had finished the first one, Terry was standing in front of him with a small tray containing three more. Claustima swapped the empty glass with one from the tray. "Runnier than the '07 but with hints of mule."

"That wouldn't be one of your jokes, Sir?"

"Indeed, Roberts. It would be."

♦

It had been a longer drive than their usual outings, but they were nearly there. Terry didn't need to peer back into the carriage to know that Claustima had been soundly asleep all the way as the contented snore advertised his state quite adequately. Terry had been alarmed at the Leader's comment about the wine, certain that he had noticed the extra ethanol he had used to spike it. But it was nothing; in his usual way, Claustima had quaffed the rare vintage like a flagon of beer and by the fourth glass could hardly tell it from grape juice and meths.

All the way, Terry had agonised over whether he was doing the right thing; torn between his duty and the very real bond he had with his charge. Claustima was only a result of Terry's own actions so he was the last person to criticise the Leader. Yes, he had his failings; but Terry considered the steep mountain the apeman had to climb to substitute for a man of breeding and honour. His progress was a testament to the work of Deborah, who had more than delivered on her promise to Mr Avery all those years ago. So now Clo's final task was to make way for the real Leader, born from stately stock to put the planet Purity on the track that was always ordained for her, And Terry's part in the succession was to make it as peaceful for Clo' as he possibly could.

Terry had practised the manoeuvre a dozen times that week, but he still felt like a complete novice. Horses are not built to walk backwards and articulated vehicles always steer the wrong way when backed up. The combination of the two had him reciprocating between slow, backwards and out of control and a short lurch forwards to try again. The result of all this to-and-fro eventually worked in Terry's favour, wearing a pair of rough channels through the apex he was trying to navigate. Suddenly, for no apparent reason, it all came together and the carriage rolled smoothly back down the grooves. Terry had to act quickly to stop the horses before they also reached the down-slope. He jumped down and patted Cadiz on the shoulder; Jerez always followed her lead, so both horses calmed quickly. A carrot each from his pocket and they were content to stand there.

Satisfied that he now wouldn't get kicked in the head, Terry crawled behind the horses and pulled the locking clip from the coupling on the carriage. A loop of the rope they always kept under the driver's seat went through the clevis pin, then up to the window and fed through to where Clo' was sleeping. Terry then joined Clo' in the back seat of the carriage, carefully closing and latching the door behind him.

Glasses and bottles were strewn around the front seat amongst the uneaten food. Terry selected a cleanish glass and the half full bottle still protected with a cork and arranged them in a small cleared space. Half of the ground-up sleeping pills from his pocket went into the glass before he swirled it around with wine and sat back with his Leader. "Clo', we are here." But Claustima didn't stir. Terry put a protecting arm around him and settled there sipping his "lotion with the potion" with the rope ready for one final tug.

Purity Year 25, day 125

Deborah had to admit, Francis May had done an outstanding job with his genetic tinkering. The boy in the middle of the crowd of five-year-olds was the spitting image of his noble uncle at that age (vault-born leaders were always referred to as the nephew of their predecessor). She wondered what Terry would have made of the boy, outwardly just like Clo' yet so different. Her mind wandered back to those days when her soulmate was still alive and the fateful day when everything changed.

They say that Terry Roberts did his best, trying everything to escape from the treacherous sandy bank. If only he had let the coachman drive that day, maybe Watkins' expertise might have allowed the horses to gain some purchase and pull them out. But their doom was finally sealed by the heroic sacrifice of Claustima Baines-Crackpole II, First Leader. By pulling the coupling pin from the coach, he allowed his beloved white mares to scramble to safety while the coach and its two occupants slid backwards into the tar pit, never to be seen again.

Victoria Berengar had raised some doubts about how the Leader had reached the coupling from way back in the coach, but everyone agreed that no mere butler was capable of the heroism shown by Claustima that day. Deborah was quietly in agreement with Miss Berengar, Terry would always be her hero.

"By Goethe! He's doing it again!" Deborah rushed down to the litter of children. "Stop that Tim', those are your toys."

Two of the children had already made good their escape, clutching exquisite stuffed copies of Old Earth animals. Claustima Baines-Crackpole III (or Tim) stopped with a penguin extended for another small boy. The boy saw Deborah approaching, snatched the bird and ran for the cedar trees. She pushed the waiting queue back and faced Claustima. "You mustn't let them bully you, Tim'. Those are your toys."

Claustima was confused. "Not bully, Aya. I am Leader."

Poor thing, how they take advantage of him. "Leaders don't have to do what others tell them Tim'. They are your toys."

Claustima nodded with a satisfied look. "My toys." He picked up a black and white striped horse and handed it to a girl wearing a primrose coloured dress.

Deborah was too quick for both of them and intercepted the gift. "If you give them away, you won't get any more."

This required some thought from Claustima. He paused with his brow furrowed then lightened into a sunny smile. "Okay." and went for the horse again.

Deborah was exasperated. *If only he had inherited some of his uncle's intelligence. This one is a complete dunce!* She stopped, horrified at the thought. Guilt washed over her. *Clo' was descended from apemen, he was the dunce. Tim' is a real Leader and I should treat his wishes with the reverence they deserve.*

Claustima watched Deborah with profound interest. He stood and put his hand on her shoulder. "I keep toys. You be happy, Aya."

The girl in the yellow dress used the diversion as an opportunity to grab the horse. Deborah pretended not to notice.

♦

If you enjoyed this story and would like to share your thoughts with others, please leave a review. Your positive review is greatly appreciated!

About the Author

A gifted storyteller from an early age, St Clare has an easy engaging style that belies the complexity of his work.

Born in Bangalore India, the son of a third generation British Raj father and an Indian mother, St Clare was raised and educated in rural England.

In spite of his early fascination with the written word, his skill with technology led him to a successful career in systems architecture. He continued to develop his writing throughout his IT career, applying his deep knowledge of both technical structure and the intrinsic human factor to his work. He now spends his life travelling and writing full time.

The Ark Ship Short Story Series

Silversphere Media Group is proud to bring you "Apeman", the first story in Gerald St Clare's larger collection of works based on the theme of the human "Ark Ships". Please check back over the coming months for more short stories in this series. If you would like a free copy of the ebook, please join the GSC readers group here: **https://bit.ly/2Ow52Sp**

Up Coming Novels

Gerald St Clare is of the most significant science fiction writers to come along for many years, and we look forward to bring you much more of his work.

Please keep an eye out for "Saucers", St Clare's debut novel, and the first book in the "Circles Trilogy"

GERALD ST CLARE – CORE READERS GROUP

You can also become a member of St Clare's trusted core readership, and be notified of any upcoming new releases and book signings, receive the occasional pre-release manuscript along with invitations to engage directly with the author in special online interactive feedback/chat forums, please visit:

www.geraldstclare.com

www.ingramcontent.com/pod-product-compliance
Lightning Source LLC
LaVergne TN
LVHW041542060526
838200LV00037B/1106